George, Timmy and the Lighthouse Mystery

*The **Just George** series*

by Sue Welford

1 George, Timmy and the Haunted Cave

2 George, Timmy and the Curious Treasure

3 George, Timmy and the Footprint in the Sand

4 George, Timmy and the Secret in the Cellar

5 George, Timmy and the Stranger in the Storm

6 George, Timmy and the Lighthouse Mystery

George, Timmy and the Lighthouse Mystery

Sue Welford

Illustrated by Lesley Harker

A division of Hodder Headline Limited

First published in Great Britain in 2000
by Hodder Children's Books

10 9 8 7 6 5 4 3 2 1

For further information on Enid Blyton,
please contact www.blyton.com

A Catalogue record for this book is available from
the British Library

ISBN 0 340 77882 2

Typeset by Avon Dataset Ltd, Bidford-on-Avon, Warks

Printed and bound in Great Britain by
The Guernsey Press Co. Ltd, Channel Isles

Hodder Children's Books
a division of Hodder Headline Ltd
338 Euston Road
London NW1 3BH

Contents

1 Timothy goes digging 1
2 In trouble again! 13
3 Rocky Point 23
4 Capture! 32
5 Inside the lighthouse 44
6 A bright idea 54
7 Under the lamp 65
8 Making up stories? 76
9 Timmy 86
10 A puzzle 98
11 Timothy digs again 106
12 The end of the adventure 115

1

Timothy goes digging

'Oh, Timmy, what *have* you been up to now!' cried George, gazing at her pet puppy's muddy paws in horror. 'Digging a hole in Mummy's garden, I bet!'

'Wuff,' said Timothy. 'Wuff, wuff!' He gazed at George with his melting brown eyes and pricked up his ears. His shaggy tail wagged uncertainly.

When his small mistress used that stern voice he knew he was in trouble.

George looked around and, sure enough, there was a large hole underneath one of her mother's garden shrubs. She quickly scooped up handfuls of earth and filled it in, stamping on it with her plimsolls until it didn't look as if the puppy had dug a hole there at all.

'We'd better go down to the beach so you can wash the dirt off in the sea before Mummy gets back from shopping and sees you,' panted George when she had finished. She bent down and gave her puppy a big hug, so he knew she had already forgiven him for digging the hole and getting in such a mess. 'You know she'll go mad if you go indoors with dirty paws and get mud everywhere!'

'Wuff, wuff,' said Timothy again, jumping up to try to lick George's freckled nose. He knew she was never angry with him for long. The little dog was delighted that they were going down to the shore. He adored splashing about in the warm, salty blue sea. It was almost as much fun as digging a great big hole in the garden!

'Come on, then,' urged George, skipping off down the garden path towards the gate. She clapped her hands and grinned, her vivid blue eyes shining with mischief and her short, dark curls bouncing around her head. 'Let's get going before Mummy gets back from the village.'

'Wuff,' said Timothy, trotting along beside her and leaping up and down excitedly. 'Wuff, wuff!'

Through the garden gate the two little rogues went. George put her hands in the pockets of her shorts and whistled a merry tune as she skipped along the narrow path that led from the garden, over the cliff top then dropped gently down to Kirrin Bay. The bay was a curving horseshoe of golden sand. Rocky cliffs jutted out at one end and in the middle of the bay was Kirrin Island. In the middle of the island was an exciting, mysterious old stone castle. Kirrin Castle had two tumbledown towers and was one of George's favourite places in the whole world. It had belonged to her mother's family for many years and she had promised that, one day, she would give it to George all for herself.

'Race you, Tim!' cried George suddenly, taking

her hands out of her pockets and beginning to run, skip and hop down towards the shore. 'Beat you!'

'Wuff,' barked Timothy happily, setting off after her.

George and Timothy were no ordinary pair. Most of all in the world, George wanted to be a boy. Her real name was Georgina but she hated it and only answered people if they called her George. She always wore shorts and shirts and had cut her dark curls so short she looked exactly like a boy. She could climb and run and whistle and sail as good as any boy and woe betide anyone who said she could not! George had a very quick temper but, although she often flared up, she soon got over her moods. She was honest and truthful and a very loyal little girl.

She'd had Timothy since he was a tiny puppy. She had been walking on the moor one day when she had come across the small, shaggy pup hiding in the heather. She had taken him home and named him Timothy because she thought it was a brave name for a brave little fellow. When Timothy wasn't claimed, her father said she could keep him as long as he was good. Timothy had become her best friend. No-one knew exactly what type of dog he was. His coat was a shaggy brown, his head was too big, his tail too long, his paws too broad and his ears too floppy. But George didn't care one bit. He was the best and loveliest puppy in the whole world, and it was wonderful to have such a loyal friend. George didn't really have any close friends and had been quite happy to play on her own until Timothy came along. She did have three cousins who lived in London whose names were Julian, Dick and Anne, but she had never met them and didn't particularly want to. Especially as one of them was a girl!

'Here we are!' called the little tomboy as she hopped down the bank and on to the warm, golden sand. The sun sparkled on the water as she ran towards it with Timothy at her heels. 'In you go, old boy!'

Timothy barked and ran into the water. There were only little waves today, breaking with a gentle whisper on the sand. He bounced up and down, barking at the seagulls who bobbed on the surface a little distance away. Timothy hadn't yet learned to swim but he wasn't a bit scared of the water. He barked at the ripples and frolicked around until all the garden mud had washed off and his fur was clean as a whistle.

'Come on, then,' called George when she saw his coat was shiny again. 'Mummy will never know you were covered in mud. *Or* that you dug a hole in her flower bed. Let's run back. It's lunch-time and my tummy's rumbling like mad!'

Back across the sand, the two went. Up the bank and along the path to Kirrin Cottage, the house where they lived. The house was really too big to be called a cottage. It sat on top of a low cliff overlooking Kirrin Bay and had white stone walls and an old wooden front door. George had a lovely view of the sea from the side window of her little bedroom up in the roof. She loved to lie in bed at night and listen to the waves and the calling of the sea-birds across the water.

Joanna, the kindly woman who helped George's mother in the house, was in the kitchen getting lunch ready when the two hurtled in.

'That dog's all wet!' she exclaimed as Timothy

left salty paw marks across the kitchen floor. She flapped her tea-towel at him. 'Out you go before you get into trouble!'

'Wuff!' Timothy barked and tried to catch the tea-towel as Joanna flicked it at him. He jumped up and caught a corner of it in his mouth. 'Grr, grrr!' growled the little dog, shaking the material with all his might. 'Grr!'

'Goodness me!' laughed Joanna, her eyes almost disappearing in her round, jolly face as she smiled. 'You *are* fierce for such a small dog!'

'He's very fierce and very clever,' said George, laughing and trying to prise the tea-cloth from Timothy's jaws. 'Let go, you bad boy!'

'Grr,' growled Timothy, pulling even harder. He always tried to obey George but sometimes he found he simply could not! Especially when he was having such a good game.

There was a great deal of noise going on with George and Joanna laughing and Timothy growling loudly and the tea-cloth flapping around like mad.

Suddenly there came the sound of heavy footsteps thumping along the hall and George's father appeared in the doorway. His dark brows were drawn together in a fierce scowl and he looked very angry indeed. He was a very tall man with dark hair, who always seemed to be frowning. Timothy was quite scared of him.

'What *is* all this row going on?' shouted Father. 'How on earth am I expected to get any work done!' He was a famous scientist and spent many hours in his study working out important formulas. He hated being disturbed.

At last George managed to prise the tea-cloth

from Timothy's teeth. 'Sorry, Father,' she said, still giggling. 'We were only having a game.'

'Yes, I can see that,' stormed Father, eyeing the torn tea-cloth. 'For goodness sake go outside, and stay outside, George! And take that wretched dog with you. I won't tell you again.'

'But Father we've come in for something to eat,' protested George, her smile turning to such a fierce scowl that she looked *exactly* like her father. 'And Timmy isn't wretched, he's lovely!'

'Well, have a picnic down on the beach or somewhere,' said her father, turning to go back to his study. 'And do it *quietly*!'

'Yes, Father,' said George, still scowling. 'Come on, Tim, let's go back outside,' she added huffily. George often got into huffs although they never lasted for long.

'I'll pack you up a nice picnic, shall I?' asked Joanna. 'I've got some of that apple pie left that I baked yesterday.'

'Oh, yes, please,' said George, the scowl disappearing and a lovely smile taking its place. 'We'll take our picnic down to the village and watch the boats in the harbour, shall we, Timmy?'

'Wurf,' said Timothy. He adored picnics. In fact he adored doing most things if it meant he could be with George.

'And we'll say hello to Alf,' continued George. Alf was the son of a fisherman who lived in Kirrin Village. George had known Alf for many years and he was very fond of Timothy.

'Wuff,' said Timothy again. He loved visiting Alf. The boy always had a tit-bit in his pocket to be gobbled up as quickly as possible, just in case there was another one to follow.

They went outside to wait while Joanna filled George's rucksack with all manner of good things. First she made some ham sandwiches, wrapped them up and tucked them inside. Then she filled another bag with a huge piece of homemade chocolate cake, some ginger biscuits, a slice of apple pie and some juicy, purple plums picked from the orchard. Then she fetched a bottle of fizzy ginger-beer, and a packet of beefy dog chews for Timothy. She packed the whole lot into George's rucksack.

'Your picnic's ready,' called the kind woman, opening the back door. 'Come and get it!'

'Oh, thank you, Joanna,' cried George, hitching the rucksack on to her back. 'You make the best picnic in the world!'

'Get along with you,' said Joanna smiling. 'Have a nice time, both of you.'

'We shall,' called George as Timothy scampered in front of her and waited at the gate. 'See you later, Joanna!'

2

In trouble again!

Soon, the two had reached Kirrin Village and were making their way across the shingle towards the little harbour. The fleet of fishing boats was pulled high up on the beach out of the reach of the tide.

They soon found Alf, sitting on the harbour wall eating fish and chips out of newspaper.

'Mmm, that smells awfully good,' said George, sitting down beside him and shrugging off her rucksack. She loved fish and chips, especially if they were wrapped in newspaper. They always tasted better that way.

'Have some,' said Alf, holding out the fish and chips.

'It's all right, thanks,' said George. 'We've got a lovely picnic haven't we, Timmy?'

'Wuff,' said Timothy, jumping up at Alf. He loved picnics but the fish and chips smelled good too.

'Hello, old boy,' said Alf, ruffling the little dog's brown fur and giving George and Timothy a broad grin. 'Want a chip?'

'Woof,' said Timothy, sitting up to beg.

'That's clever,' said Alf, laughing and throwing one to him. 'When did he learn to do that?'

'Oh, ages ago,' said George, tucking into a ham sandwich. 'He's the cleverest dog in the world.'

'He certainly is,' said Alf. 'Well, what have you two been up to?'

'Well,' said George, sighing, 'we've been picnicking and walking and sailing and

swimming but we haven't had an adventure lately, have we, Tim?'

Timothy gave a little whine as he sat up and begged for another chip.

'And it looks as if we're not going to have one these holidays,' said George, sighing again. 'And we do love adventures, don't we, Timmy?'

'Wuff,' said Timothy, agreeing as usual.

'Well, something will turn up, I expect,' said Alf, finishing his fish and chips and folding up the newspaper. 'It usually does.'

'Hope so,' said George, her mouth full of apple pie.

Alf left the newspaper and went to have a game with Timothy, throwing a piece of driftwood for the puppy to chase after and bring back. When George had finished eating she picked up Alf's paper and took it over to the litter bin with the wrappings from her own picnic. There was a picture of a man on the front of the newspaper. An evil-looking man with shaggy black hair and a straggly beard.

The headline read: 'Prisoner escapes in bid for freedom.' George didn't like the look of the man one little bit. He had the sort of face that gave you bad dreams.

She gave a little shudder as she screwed up the paper and threw it into the bin.

She ran to join in the game and soon the three of them were having a lovely time. She and Alf threw the stick for Timothy, then laughed as he raced after it and brought it back. After a while, the puppy was tired out and lay down on the shingle, panting like a steam train, his big pink tongue lolling out.

'I'd better get on with my chores,' said Alf. 'I've got to mend some of my dad's fishing-nets. See you soon, you two,' and off he went with a wave of his hand.

'Come on, Timmy,' said George. 'Let's get home, shall we?'

Timothy soon recovered and trotted along the path beside her. When they reached Kirrin Cottage, George's mother and father were in the garden. They were both standing by one of the flower beds. Father's hands were on his hips and he looked very angry indeed.

'We can see where that dog has dug holes all

over your mother's flower border,' stormed the angry man as George and Timothy came skipping merrily down the path. 'Look!'

George skidded to a halt. Her eyes followed her father's pointing finger. There were two enormous holes in the earth and some of Mother's precious plants lay in limp tatters beside them.

Oh dear, thought George. No wonder Timmy had got so dirty that morning. He had dug *lots* of holes and not just the one she had filled in.

Timothy gave a little whine and hid behind her legs. He knew he had been naughty but this tall man called Father didn't seem to understand that sometimes dogs just couldn't help digging. Besides, he had buried a bone there somewhere and he was only trying to find it so he could have another jolly good chew at it. What was the point of having big, strong front paws if you didn't dig with them?

'I don't know what we're going to do with him,' said George's mother, shaking her head sadly. 'He really *is* a bad dog.'

'Wuff,' said Timothy softly, creeping out from

behind George's legs. He went to lick her mother's hand as if to say he was very sorry indeed.

'It's no good him doing that,' said Father angrily. 'I warned you, Georgina. If he doesn't behave we'll have to send him away.'

'You wouldn't! You couldn't!' cried George.

'Indeed, I would!' said her father. 'And maybe a good smack would do him good.'

'I don't think we need to do that, Quentin,' said her mother hastily. 'The dog just needs training, that's all.'

'It's too late for that, Fanny,' said her husband. 'He's had many chances and this is the last straw.'

'What are you going to do?' asked George, still scowling because her father had called her Georgina and because he was being very unreasonable. Timothy was a puppy. Puppies liked digging and that was that.

'I'm going to telephone PC Moon at the police station and ask him to find him a new home,' said her father. 'Until then he'll have to be tied up.'

'No!' said George angrily. 'I won't let him be tied up! And I *won't* let him go to a new home!'

She picked Timothy up and held him close. 'He's my best friend! You can't send your best friend away!'

'I don't care what he is,' said her father, still frowning angrily. 'I don't know why you can't have human beings as friends like other people, Georgina. There are lots of nice girls in the village you could play with.'

'I hate girls,' scowled George stormily. 'And I hate human beings.'

Her father sighed and shook his head. He loved his fierce little daughter very much but she could be extremely stubborn at times. 'How can I possibly be expected to do my work with all this fuss going on,' he said, storming back indoors. 'Sort it out, will you, Fanny!' He stomped along to his study at the other end of the house. They heard his door slam so hard the whole of Kirrin Cottage seemed to shake.

'Don't worry, George,' said her mother, sighing and putting her arm round her daughter. 'He won't remember to phone PC Moon.' George's father was always forgetting things and this time George hoped what her mother said was true.

'He might,' she said, trying very hard indeed not to cry. She hated people who cried. She thought it was babyish and silly and was determined never to do it. But this time she could hardly help a tear coming to her eye. She brushed it away angrily and hoped that her mother hadn't noticed.

'Well, we'll cross that bridge when we come to it,' said her poor mother gently. 'But you really must keep Timmy under control, darling. Otherwise I'm afraid he really *will* have to go.'

George shook off her mother's arm. 'Well, I won't let him be tied up and I won't let him go to another home,' cried the angry little girl. 'Father can go and boil his head!'

And, with that, she marched off down the garden path with Timothy tucked under her arm like a shaggy brown parcel.

'Where are you going?' called her mother anxiously. She knew that once George went off in a huff she might be gone for hours.

'For a walk!' shouted George. 'Somewhere where Father won't shout at us!'

3

Rocky Point

George marched along the path with Timothy at her heels. He felt very sober. He had been the cause of a big argument and felt very unhappy that his mistress was so upset.

But soon the little dog forgot all about it. He spotted a score of white bobbing tails scattering in front of him. Rabbits! What fun to chase them!

'Wuff,' barked Timothy happily, bounding off after them. 'Wuff, wuff!' Life was grand when there were bunnies to chase!

'Don't you dare catch any,' called George, still feeling angry and upset. 'Or you'll be in *my* bad books too.'

She strode along the path at a fearsome rate, her head down and her plimsolls going clump, clump angrily on the path. Before she knew it they had passed Kirrin Farm and the tumble-down Kitswold Mill. The path widened into a rocky descent that went right down the cliff to a lighthouse at the bottom.

'Let's go and explore,' said George, when she saw the lighthouse, feeling surprised they had come so far. 'I haven't brought you here before, Timmy. It's jolly exciting.' She forgot she was in a bad mood as she scrambled down the track, with Timothy slipping and sliding in front of her. Their footsteps started a small landslide and a shower of rocks and stones tumbled in front of them, gathering speed as they went. They crackled and bounced on the rocks below.

Soon the two were standing on the little beach

at the base of the cliff staring at the lighthouse. It was built on a rocky outcrop a few metres out into the sea and was surrounded by horrid, sharp, pointed rocks which would make a hole in any ship that came too close.

There was a large notice saying: 'Danger, Keep Out'.

'It's called Rocky Point Lighthouse,' explained George, above the noise of the waves crashing against the boulders. 'No-one ever comes here. You can only get to it when the tide goes out. It hasn't been used for years. There's another one just round the bay, close to Demon's Rocks, so they don't really need this one. Isn't it exciting?' She jumped up on to one of the rocks, chuckling with delight as a huge wave broke close by and splashed her with salty spray.

'Wuff,' said Timothy, backing off a little. The waves looked white and angry as they surged over the rocks and he didn't want to get washed away.

The little dog stared up at the tall, narrow building with the round, glass tower at the top. It had once been painted red and white but the colour had been worn off by the wind and weather. It really was the oddest house he had ever seen. The bottom of it was buried deep into the rocks and a flight of seaweedy, slippery, stone steps led up to a great, rusty iron door above the height of the thundering surf. It was sealed with planks and a huge padlock and chain and looked as if it hadn't been opened for years.

'It was built to warn sailors about these beastly sharp rocks,' said George, hopping on to another rock. 'And in the olden days people called wreckers used to shine lights in the wrong place so ships hit the rocks and sank.'

'Wuff,' said Timothy.

'Then, when the cargo floated ashore, the bad people used to steal it,' explained George. 'Wasn't that a horrid thing to do?'

'Wuff,' said Timothy, agreeing that indeed it was a dreadful thing to do.

'And up there,' said George, pointing to the very top of the lighthouse. 'Is where the real lighthouse men used to light the lamps to warn ships of the danger. I'd love to be a lighthouse keeper, wouldn't you, Timmy? There wouldn't be any grown-ups to tell us what to do!'

'Wuff,' said Timothy, not sounding at all sure. There wouldn't be any gardens to dig holes in either if you lived in a lighthouse!

'Let's wait until the tide goes out,' said George. 'Then we can see if we can get inside and explore.'

Timothy gave a small whine. How were they going to get through a padlocked door? He looked up. There were three windows going up the side of the building but even the lowest one looked too high up to climb through. He

scrambled back to the beach and sat down feeling rather puzzled. George would find a way in if she possibly could. Once his determined little mistress got a bee in her bonnet she never gave up.

George followed him, jumping from rock to rock then sitting down beside him. Overhead, gulls wheeled and dived above the waves and the air was full of the smell of the sea.

They settled back to wait for the tide to go out. It was warm in the sunshine and George began to feel rather sleepy. They had walked a very long way indeed. Her tummy began to rumble and her mouth watered as she thought of Joanna's delicious homemade chocolate cake they had eaten for their lunchtime picnic. If she hadn't gone off in such a huff then she would have thought to bring some with her.

'I suppose we'll have to go back sooner or later,' she said to Timothy, sighing. 'Perhaps Father *will* forget about telephoning PC Moon.'

Timothy gave a hopeful little whine and looked up at her from under his shaggy eyebrows.

'And you must promise never to dig up Mummy's flowers again, Timmy, darling,' said

George, waggling her finger at him.

'Wuff, wuff,' said Timothy, ready to promise anything if it meant he could stay at Kirrin Cottage.

It wasn't long before the tide had gone out enough for them to reach the stone steps of the lighthouse.

'Be careful, Timmy,' cried George as they scrambled over the rocks and reached the first step. 'They're very slippery.' She clutched hold of the rusty handrail as she clambered up to the iron door. Timmy slipped and slithered behind her. Once, she had to grab him to stop him sliding off on to the rocks below.

When they reached the door, George rattled the chain. 'Oh, dear, Timmy, we're never going to get in this way. I wonder if there's another entrance?' said the daring little girl. 'Let's go round the other side.'

There was a wide ledge all the way round the outside of the building and together the two stepped carefully on to it. The sides were covered with scratchy limpets and the ledge was very slippery with slimy green seaweed. Not far below, the sea was a tumult of waves surging against the rocks.

'There's a window up there,' said George, shaking her head. 'But it's much too high to get through. Oh, blow, Timmy, I really wanted to explore, didn't you?'

But Timothy wasn't listening. Above the sound of the waves, his sharp ears had caught the sound of something else. The sound of voices. Two people were coming down the rocky path towards them. George had said nobody ever came there. So, who on earth could it be?

4

Capture!

'What's wrong, Timmy?' asked George anxiously, when she saw that the puppy's ears were pricked up and he was quivering with excitement. 'What can you hear?'

'Grr,' said Timothy, growling deep in his throat. 'Grr.'

George turned round and saw the two figures

scrambling down the steep path towards the lighthouse.

'Oh, blow!' she exclaimed. 'Who on earth is that? Quick, Timmy, let's hide before they see us. We're not supposed to be here, you know. If it's the coastguard we'll be in trouble.'

The two scrambled back to the steps and, quickly running down, they jumped off the bottom one and crouched behind a large rock. Timothy was still growling fiercely. Luckily the sound was drowned out by the noise of the waves.

'Ssh,' whispered George, putting her hand gently over his muzzle. 'Or they'll hear you! We'll be in real trouble if we're spotted.'

The two men had reached the rocks and were walking across towards the lighthouse steps.

'Bit slippery here, Max,' said the taller of the two in a deep voice. 'Better be careful.'

George peeped out and saw the other figure almost slip and fall into the water, his arms waving like a windmill. The taller one, who was dark haired and had a beard, grabbed his arm.

'Take it easy, Max,' he said. 'If you break your

neck we'll never find those diamonds.'

'Diamonds?' whispered George. 'What on earth is he talking about?' She could see the man clearly, looming very close to her hiding place. She gasped. He looked familiar but she couldn't think why. She racked her brains, frowning. Where *had* she seen that face before?

By now, Max had climbed the steps and was standing in front of the iron door with a scowl on his face. He was younger than the first man, dressed in dark trousers and a rather grubby vest with no sleeves. 'I don't know how we're going to get in,' he said, rattling the heavy chain. 'This is locked up good and proper. Doesn't look as if it's been used for years.'

'Of course it hasn't,' snapped the bigger man. 'That's why Pete hid the diamonds here, because he knew they wouldn't be found.'

In her hiding place, George gasped again. There were diamonds hidden in the old lighthouse. How very thrilling!

'All right, then, Dave, you try,' she heard Max say sourly. 'You're supposed to be the strong one.' He stood back while the bigger man rattled the

chain and pulled at the padlock.

'You're right,' said Dave, shaking his head. 'Pete must have got in another way.'

Crouched behind the rock George frowned even harder. Who was Pete? And why had he hidden some diamonds in the old lighthouse? Then her heart began to pound furiously. She had suddenly realised where she had seen the man named Dave. It was his picture in the newspaper wrapped around Alf's fish and chips.

Dave was an escaped convict!

'Look,' said Dave, suddenly pointing upwards. 'Up there! A window. I bet he got in that way.'

The two men stared up at the small window above their heads.

'Yes, you're right,' said Max. 'Pete climbs like a monkey. *And* he's small enough to get through. Neither of us could. What do you reckon we should do?'

'No idea,' said Dave, shaking his head. 'Even if we got a ladder we couldn't get in. If Pete wasn't in prison I'd send him up there, all right. Sneaky little blighter. If he hadn't let on to someone else where he'd hidden the diamonds we'd never have found out. I'd love to see his face if we find 'em and when he gets out of prison and comes to get them, they're gone!'

He sat down on the steps with a dark frown on his face. From her hiding place, George could see his piercing eyes and gave a little shudder. It was the first time she had ever been close to an escaped prisoner – and a diamond thief at that!

'Yes,' said Max, giving a sly grin. 'It would serve him right!'

'But that doesn't solve anything right now,' said

Dave, still frowning. 'We've got to get in that window somehow if it kills us.'

'Probably will,' said Max, gazing at the waves smashing against the rocks. 'I wouldn't fancy falling down there. I bet there's crabs and all sorts in those rocks. There might even be sharks.'

How silly, thought George who knew all about the wildlife that lived in the sea around Kirrin Bay. *Everyone* knows there aren't any sharks here!

By now, Timothy was quivering with anger. It was all getting too much to bear. How dare these horrid humans come barging in and spoil their fun! He could see a trouser leg flapping very close to his nose and was longing to get it between his teeth. If he could grab it then it might scare them away and he and his small mistress could carry on enjoying themselves.

Suddenly he could stand it no longer. He simply *had* to get that cloth between his teeth! He lunged away from George's grasp and grabbed the trouser leg.

'Grr,' he said, shaking it fiercely. 'Grr, grrr.'

'Hey!' yelled the man, falling back in surprise. 'Help! Dave, something's got me!'

'Blimey, it's a dog!' shouted Dave, kicking out at Timothy. 'Where did he come from?' He kicked out again, narrowly missing sending Timothy flying into the water.

'Don't you kick my dog,' shouted George, springing from her hiding place. 'He's only having a game. Leave him alone!'

'A game!' shouted Max, trying to dislodge Timothy's very sharp teeth from his trouser leg. 'Some game! Get off, will you!'

'Timmy, leave!' commanded George, scared Timothy would get hurt as a kick almost caught him in the ribs. 'Leave!'

Timothy let go immediately and stood growling at Max. He didn't like the look of these two humans one little bit. They had loud voices and smelled funny. His doggie instinct told him that the one with the piercing eyes was very dangerous indeed.

'Look what he's done,' exclaimed Max. 'He's torn my trousers. He deserves a good hiding!' He lunged towards Timothy but George was quicker. She grabbed the puppy and picked him up.

'Don't you dare touch him!' she said fiercely,

her vivid eyes glowing with anger. 'Or I'll . . . I'll . . .' She was so furious at the thought of someone trying to kick Timothy that she couldn't think *what* she would do if they hurt him.

Dave laughed, throwing back his huge head, his beard waggling. 'All right, sonny,' he said. 'You'd better get going and take that mutt with you!'

'Come on, Timmy, let's go home,' said George haughtily, rather scared of this huge man who she knew had escaped from prison. She was too frightened to be pleased he thought she was a boy. Her mind was whizzing. If they could get home quickly and tell Father they had seen the escaped prisoner he could phone PC Moon and the police would come and catch him.

The sooner the dangerous man was back behind bars, the better!

George put Timothy down and the two began to scramble back towards the beach. George's heart was pounding furiously. It was quite a long way back to Kirrin Cottage. They must hurry, hurry!

But as they started to race towards the steep

cliff path, George heard heavy footsteps and felt a big, strong hand on her shoulder.

'Wait a minute, son,' came the deep voice of Dave from behind her. 'We've got a little job for you.'

'What kind of a job?' asked George, turning quickly. Timothy had been running on ahead. He stopped and turned and came scampering back when he saw his mistress had been grabbed by the man.

'A little climbing job,' said Dave, marching George firmly back towards the lighthouse. Timothy ran along beside her, barking at the man's booted feet. Dave kicked out suddenly, catching Timothy in the ribs and bowling him over and over.

'Hey!' shouted George, struggling like mad to get free of the man's heavy hand. 'You leave my dog alone!'

Timothy scrambled to his feet and shook himself. His ribs were bruised and he felt rather dizzy. He staggered back towards George. He only had one thought in his mind and that was to save his mistress.

Suddenly Max darted forward and scooped him up, holding him tightly, one arm over his small, shaggy body, the other firmly round his neck. Timothy growled and snarled but he couldn't wriggle free.

'Put him down!' yelled George, still wriggling and trying to kick her captor. 'He'll bite you!'

But Timothy was held firmly in the man's grasp. He tried to struggle but it hurt too much. He gave a little whine deep in his throat. He could see the human with a beard marching George up to the lighthouse. She was shouting and struggling and kicking but couldn't get away.

The little dog's heart turned over in fear as the man holding him found a piece of old rope on the beach and tied it to his collar. He put him down and looped the other end of the rope round a rock. 'Stay there, you scruffy mutt,' he growled. 'Your little master is about to become a monkey and if he refuses then things are going to look pretty bad for both of you! So he'd better do as he's told!'

Timothy lunged bravely at the man, barking fiercely, but every move hurt his ribs, especially

when the rope jerked him back savagely. He gave a little whine and lay down painfully on the stones. He put his nose between his paws and whined again. He felt stiff and sore all over. George was standing at the top of the lighthouse steps and the human with the beard was pointing up to the window.

'Up there,' said Dave. 'You're small enough to climb through that window.'

'Not likely,' said George, shaking her head defiantly. 'Even if I could get through, it's miles too high.'

'Not if you stand on my shoulders,' said Dave, grabbing hold of her again. 'Now do as you're told or you'll never see that dog of yours again!'

5

Inside the lighthouse

George knew that the horrible man meant every word he said. If she didn't climb up through the window, some dreadful harm would come to Timothy. The brave little girl had no choice but to do as she was told.

'Very well, then,' she said sulkily. 'What do you want me to do when I'm inside?'

'Look for a package,' said Max. 'A box, probably wrapped up in cloth or paper.'

'What kind of a box?' asked George even though she realised the villain meant a box of diamonds because she had heard them discussing it earlier.

'Never you mind,' said Dave. 'You just get it and bring it out.' He grabbed hold of George and marched her across to the foot of the steps. He pushed and pulled her round the ledge until the little window was above them. 'Now,' he snarled. 'Up on my shoulders, you!'

He lifted George up until she was standing on his broad shoulders. She wobbled around for a second or two and was scared she would fall on to the rocks below. When she found her balance she looked up. The man was right. Now she was standing on his shoulders, the window was within easy reach.

'Go on!' called Max. 'Get a move on! We haven't got all day.'

She reached upwards cautiously and tried the window catch. It was rusty and stiff but, to her great relief, opened with a hard push.

'Inside with you!' called Max.

George pulled herself up on to the window-sill and scrambled through the open window. There was a long drop the other side into a room stacked full of smelly, old oil cans and brown cardboard boxes. It seemed miles down there.

'Oh well,' she thought to herself as she launched herself off the window ledge. 'Here goes!'

The little girl landed heavily and lay winded for a minute or two. One leg was twisted painfully underneath her. She winced as she straightened it out.

'Ouch!' she said, rubbing the bruise, biting her lip, determined *not* to cry. She staggered to her feet. She must hurry and find the box quickly so that the men would let Timothy go.

Outside, the two scoundrels were still shouting at her.

'What's in there? Any sign of the package?' one of them yelled.

'Oh, shut up!' she said out loud. She knew they couldn't hear her but saying something rude made her feel better. Her voice echoed round the strange room and bounced back at her. 'I'm being as quick as I can!' she shouted for good measure.

George limped to the centre of the round room and looked around. The oil cans and provisions must have been left there when the lighthouse was abandoned.

'This must have been a store room,' she said, speaking aloud to keep up her spirits. 'How on earth am I supposed to find a box of diamonds amongst all this?'

It was very dim in there, and rather eerie. The only light came from the small window George had clambered through. The sound of the waves breaking over the rocks below was like the roar of thunder beneath her feet.

An iron, spiral staircase went up through the centre of the room to the next floor. George rummaged through the boxes. They contained rusty tins of baked beans, sardines, tins of corned beef. She came across some boxes of candles and packets of matches, rather damp from being stored so long. But nothing looked at all like a package of jewels.

'I'd better go and look on the next floor,' she

said, clambering up the spiral stairs to the next level. Outside she could still hear the men shouting instructions at her. Now and then there came a bark from Timothy and her heart turned over. She had to find the box and get back to him as quickly as she could!

The second room contained only an old settee shaped like a banana to fit in the round room. A few ancient magazines and newspapers lay on a low table, curled and yellow with age. There was an old paraffin stove next to a mouldy looking armchair. She looked underneath the sofa and chair but there was nothing there, only layers of dust and dirt. Her heart was racing. Supposing she couldn't find the box and the men were so angry they hurt Timothy? She swallowed back the tears that threatened to spill down her cheeks. She had to hurry!

Up the iron staircase George ran and out into the glass tower at the top of Rocky Point Lighthouse. A balcony of rusted iron railings ran all the way round the outside.

'This must be the lamp room,' said George, gazing at the circle of huge, high mirrors that reflected the glow from the old oil lamp in the centre. When the lamp was lit they would send the light shining out to warn ships of danger. 'I remember Father telling me how the mirrors used to turn round the light like a roundabout to make it look as if it was flashing on and off and could be seen for miles out to sea,' she muttered to herself. She tried to push the mirrors round but the mechanism was rusty and they wouldn't budge an inch.

But there was no time to think any more about things like that, or to stand and admire the thrilling view from the top of the tower. George had only one thing on her mind. To find the box the villains were after and rescue Timothy as quickly as she could.

The little girl ran round and round frantically, bending to peer into the little dark space beneath the lamp. *That* would be a good place to hide something if it was small enough. But there was nothing there. She ran back down the staircase to the lighthouse keeper's lounge, then back to the store room. Her eye fell upon a candle box. It was made of metal to keep the candles dry.

'Hmm,' said the little girl, frowning thoughtfully. 'If I wrap this up in lots of paper they might *think* it's the jewels.'

She grabbed the box of candles and raced back up to the lounge. She wrapped it up in several layers of old newspaper then ran back down the stairs. She ripped the string off one of the boxes of provisions and quickly tied it round the paper, tying the knots very tightly indeed so they would be difficult to undo.

She dragged a box over to the window and jumped up on to it. 'I've got it,' she shouted,

standing on tiptoe so that she could just see out.

'You sure?' shouted Dave, standing on the rocks below and gazing up at her.

'Honestly,' said George, keeping her fingers crossed. She hated telling lies but this time she simply had to. If she didn't make the men believe she had found the diamonds she might never see Timothy again.

'Chuck it down, then,' called Max. 'We'll catch it.'

'You let my dog go first,' shouted George, waving the package out of the window. '*Then* you can have it.' She craned her neck but couldn't see Timothy anywhere.

'Just throw it down, son,' called Max. 'Otherwise you'll be sorry.'

He had such a horrid tone to his voice that George was left in no doubt. All she could hope for was that they kept their end of the bargain and let Timothy go as soon as they had the package.

'Here it comes, then,' she shouted, holding the package out and dropping it. She saw Dave lunge forward and catch it as it fell, then she heard them cheer.

'Thanks, son, you've done a good job,' called Max. The next thing she saw was both of them clambering across the rocks and on to the beach. They hurried away, up the rocky path, over the cliff top and out of sight.

'Hey!' shouted George at the very top of her voice. 'I can't get out on my own. Hey! Come back!' She jumped up and down frantically, then went to heave another box over to the window. She put it on top of the first one then stood on them both. She could see better now, right down to the rocks. The wind had risen and huge waves were surging round them in a spray of white foam.

But there was nothing else to see.

No villains and no Timothy.

'Timmy!' yelled the desperate little girl. 'Timmy! Where are you?'

But there was no answering bark.

Timothy had completely disappeared.

6

A bright idea

George jumped off the box and dragged another one over to the window. She heaved it on top of the others and climbed up. Perhaps if she piled several on top of one another she would be able to get out?

But even when there were four boxes stacked on top of one another and she could clamber up on the sill, it was far too big a drop on the other side. If she jumped she would crash down on the rocks and probably break her neck. She had to think of something else.

George left the boxes and hurtled down to the ground floor. Maybe there would be a way to open the door from the inside? She skidded to a halt, staring at the huge iron bolts. Then she shook her head sadly as she saw there was no way she could open it from the inside. Even if she *could* slide the heavy bolts across, the padlock and chain outside would stop the door opening.

With a sigh, she ran back up the stairs, then up to the lamp room right at the top of the lighthouse. She was feeling desperately anxious and unhappy. Where *could* Timothy have gone?

'Timmy! Timmy!' she shouted, banging on the glass. 'Where are you?'

But there was no answering bark from below. The only sounds were the waves thundering round the rocks and the cries of the seagulls as they skimmed the foamy crests.

The view from the top of the lighthouse was marvellous. George could see right over the heaving, dark, blue sea to the horizon. The wave tips were touched with gold from the setting sun. The light was fading fast and it would soon be dark. She gave a shiver at the thought of spending the night all alone in the lighthouse.

'Mummy will be wondering where we've got to,' wailed the little girl to herself. 'If I'm not back by dark she'll be frantic. What *am* I going to do?' She wandered round and round, her mind spinning. The wind had become wilder still. It seemed to make strange, ghostly noises as it rattled around the top of the tower. The tide was right up to the rocks. Great breakers were surging across them in a fury of white spray. The whole building shook and shivered every time a wave broke against it, as if it might collapse at any moment. Whatever happened George couldn't get back to dry land until the tide had gone out. It looked as if she was there for the night. She bit her lip, determined not to be frightened. The lighthouse had withstood many a raging storm and was not likely to fall down right at that moment.

'I'm not sure I would have wanted to be a

lighthouse keeper after all, though,' George said to herself, going back down to the lounge and sitting forlornly on the funny-shaped settee. 'It must have been very strange and lonely all by yourself. Especially in bad weather.'

She bit her lip, feeling very close to tears again, in spite of her determination not to be scared. What *had* happened to poor Timothy? If he was lying hurt somewhere he would wonder why she didn't come to rescue him. She had never let him down and he would be unhappy and scared all alone out there.

She took a deep breath and squared her shoulders. Crying simply wouldn't do any good. Boys didn't cry and she wasn't going to either. She *had* to think of a plan.

Outside, the water thundered against the rocks as the wind rose higher and higher. Sometimes the waves splashed up so far that spray spattered against the window.

'Those lighthouse keepers must have been jolly brave,' she said out loud. 'Keeping the light going in all weathers to warn ships of the danger.'

Then, suddenly, she had a bright idea. If lights were lit to warn ships of danger, maybe *she* could light the light to tell people she was there. Someone was bound to see it and come to rescue her!

Feeling suddenly full of hope and excitement, the brave little girl ran back up the stairs to the lamp room. She peered at the huge lamp set in the circle of polished mirrors. There was a strong smell of paraffin oil and she could see a wick sticking up in the centre.

'It looks like the old oil stove that my grandfather used to have when Mummy was a little girl living at Kirrin Farm,' she said, remembering her mother telling her that grandfather's study was heated by such a thing. 'The wick was soaked in oil and you lit it with a match then put the lid back on. It used to give out light as well as heat. I bet this works in the same way.'

Back down the stairs George hurried as fast as her legs would carry her. There were cans of oil in the store room. If she could carry one up the stairs and fill the lamp then she could light it!

Soon, she was heaving a can of smelly oil up to the lamp room. She quickly poured some into a hole in the side of the lamp then looked for a knob to turn up the wick. Ah . . . there it was, sticking out at the side! She turned it carefully and in the centre of the lamp the wick rose higher and higher.

'Now,' she said, standing back with her hands on her hips. 'Matches.'

She remembered seeing some in the store room and ran quickly back down the stairs to fetch them.

Soon she was back in the lamp room with a

large box of matches clutched in her hand. She took one out. It felt damp and soft and with a sinking heart she felt sure it wouldn't light. She tried to strike it but nothing happened. There wasn't a single spark and the match broke in her fingers. She tried again and again until she saw there was only one match left in the box.

'Please light,' she murmured under her breath. 'Please light!'

To her great relief, as she struck it very hard indeed, the match caught and flared. She held it carefully over the wick. 'There,' she panted as the oil began to burn with a warm, blue flame. She turned the wick up slightly and suddenly the room was full of such a brilliant light she had to screw up her eyes against the glare.

'Oh, wonderful,' cried the little girl, clapping her hands with glee. 'It works! Hurrah!' She carefully closed the little door in front of the wick and tried to push the mechanism that drove the mirrors. It was still stuck fast. No matter how hard she pushed it wouldn't move. Not only was it rusted up but there was something stuck in the cogs, preventing it moving round.

'I'm sure it won't really matter if the light doesn't flicker on and off,' panted George, giving up and going to look out of the window. 'Someone will be bound to see it.'

Outside, a long, bright beam of light streamed out into the darkness. It seemed to stretch for miles and miles, as far as the eye could see.

'Please see it, someone, and come to rescue me soon,' whispered George. It was most thrilling to think that people in Kirrin would see the old light shining again. They would be very puzzled indeed and soon come to investigate. What a surprise they would have to find her in the lighthouse!

George went back down to the sitting-room to wait. The wind had almost blown itself out and the sea was calmer. She felt cold and shivery. She found some candles and another box of matches. The flickering light from the old candles threw strange shadows around the walls of the room when she lit them. It felt very eerie indeed to be alone in the lighthouse with the sea thundering below and the broad, bright beam of light shining to the horizon. George certainly *was* having an adventure – although she wasn't sure she was enjoying it at all.

'I hope I don't have to wait very long,' she said anxiously to herself, huddling up on the sofa and hugging herself to try to keep warm. 'And I wish I could make myself a nice hot cup of tea,' she said, thinking of the warm, cosy kitchen at home and the smell of Joanna's homemade bread baking in the oven. This made her tummy rumble and she began to feel very hungry.

'Please hurry, someone,' she said out loud. 'Please hurry!'

In fact, it wasn't very long at all before George heard voices calling from below. Had help come sooner than expected?

Full of excitement, she rushed down to the store room and jumped up on the boxes to look out of the window. Now at last she could be rescued and begin to search for Timothy.

But, to George's horror, it wasn't the coastguard or someone from the village who had come to rescue her. Or even Mummy and Father looking up anxiously at the old lighthouse. Through the fading light she could see it was the diamond thieves, standing on the rocks and looking very angry indeed! The sea was surging round their feet. Luckily, it was still far too rough for them to cross to the lighthouse.

George had a horrible feeling she knew what had happened. They had discovered she had thrown them an old candle box instead of the jewels and had come back for the real thing.

Now what was she going to do?

7

Under the lamp

'Are you still in there, sonny?' shouted Dave, glaring up at the window.

'Of course I'm still here,' yelled George. 'You know I can't get out on my own.'

'Did you light that light?' shouted Max, shaking his fist angrily.

'Yes, of course I did,' shouted George. 'I want

to be rescued. What have you done with Timmy? Bring him back at once!'

'Never you mind about that mutt,' called Max. 'You thought you'd fool us with that package but we soon found out it was the wrong one. You'd better find the real box of diamonds and throw them out.'

'Only if I can see Timmy's all right,' shouted George, standing on the boxes and staring at the two angry men beneath.

Max bent down and picked something up from beside his feet. It was Timothy, struggling and whining to be put down. He had heard his mistress shouting from inside the strange building and was longing to see her. He had been carted off by these men after George had thrown something down to them. He had struggled and tried to bite them but they had shouted at him and wouldn't let him go. When they had got to the top of the cliff they had run across the moor to a car but had soon come hurrying back when they opened the package and discovered it wasn't the jewels. They had shouted angrily and hauled him all the way back to the lighthouse, arguing

angrily between themselves all the way there.

'Here's your dog,' shouted Max. 'We took him with us thinking he'd make a good hostage if we were caught.'

'Timmy!' cried George. 'Timmy, darling! Are you all right?' She banged her fist angrily on the window-sill, furious that she couldn't get out and give him the biggest hug in the world.

Timothy whined and struggled harder in the man's arms and tried to bite his hand. Max dropped him on the ground, still hanging on to the rope attached to his collar. Timothy tried to lunge away but the man pulled him back cruelly.

'You'd better find those diamonds this time,' shouted Dave.

'If I do, you've got to promise to help me get out of here,' called George. She had hoped that some rescuers would be there by now but there was still no sign of anyone.

'*We're* calling the shots here,' yelled Dave. 'Get the diamonds now – or you'll never see your puppy again!'

George's mind raced. She had to find the diamonds and save Timothy. That was the most important thing. She was sure someone *would* see the light and come to investigate sooner or later. It seemed best to take one thing at a time. She scowled helplessly. There was nothing she could do but hunt for the jewels again, although she had no idea where they could be. She had already looked everywhere.

The man who was in prison had really hidden them well. This time, though, she had to find them. Timothy's life was at stake!

'All right,' she yelled. 'You win. I'll search again.' She jumped off the boxes and rummaged around the store room, pushing boxes and cans aside in her frantic search. Nothing. Up the spiral staircase she rushed, into the lounge, tossing aside the settee cushions and pushing her hands down the sides in case the box was there. Still nothing. She stood back, scratching her head. Where *could* the thief have hidden the jewels? There was only one more place to search. The lamp room.

Up the next flight of stairs, the desperate girl rushed. All there was in the lamp room was the lamp. Surely the jewels couldn't be hidden up there?

She stood in front of the brilliant light, shielding her eyes from the glare, frowning and biting her lip. Then she suddenly had an idea. She had tried to push the mechanism that turned the mirrors. It was terribly rusty but there was something else. Something had been preventing it from moving.

'I wonder . . .' she said, frowning and bending to peer underneath. 'I wonder . . . ?' She pushed her hand into the side, stretching her fingers out as far as they could go. They came into contact with a square box wrapped in some kind of soft material.

She grasped the package and pulled. Her heart beat with excitement, for there in her hands lay a box wrapped in a soft brown bag clasped together at the top with a gold cord. She undid the knot and drew out a velvet box with a brass clasp. She opened the lid. She gasped as she saw what lay inside: a necklace of dazzling diamonds. The very thing the thieves wanted before they would let Timmy go.

'Golly!' exclaimed George, drawing in her breath and gazing at the jewels. 'They must be worth a fortune! No wonder those horrid men are desperate to get them.'

The necklace was beautiful. Two heavy rows of sparkling crystal caught the light from the lamp like a million stars. 'I'd better get going,' said George under her breath, closing the box and wrapping it up again. She rushed down the two flights of stairs as fast as her legs would carry her.

'I've found them,' she shouted, jumping up on the boxes to look out of the window. 'Here they are!' She waved the box at the two men below.

'Are you sure it's them?' shouted Max.

'Yes!' called George. 'Shall I throw them out?'

Below, the two men said something to one another that she could not hear above the crashing of the waves against the rocks.

'We'd better wait until the sea calms down,' called Dave. 'We don't want them landing at the bottom of the ocean.'

'Someone will have seen the light and come to rescue me by then,' shouted George. 'And they'll capture you and take you back to prison! So you'd better have them now!'

The two men spoke to one another again.

George saw the big man, Dave, give Max a push towards the rocks. The smaller man had put Timothy down on the stones and the little dog had run off, the rope dragging behind him as he scuttled up the path and out of sight.

'Come back, Timmy!' yelled George, as she saw his shaggy tail disappearing into the twilight. 'Please, come back!'

'Never mind about him,' called Dave. 'He won't go far. We can soon find him and get rid of him if we don't get those diamonds.'

George's heart turned over in fear when she heard those words. The horrid man was right. Timothy wouldn't go far knowing his mistress was in grave danger even if it meant he was in danger himself.

'Max is going to try to get to the steps,' shouted Dave, grabbing Max's arm and shoving him forward. 'Then you can drop the box down to him. All right, kid?'

'I'll try,' shouted George.

'I'm not going,' said Max, looking very scared indeed. 'Those waves are massive and I can't even swim.'

'You'd better,' threatened Dave, shaking Max's arm and squeezing it so hard the smaller man winced with pain. 'If you don't you won't get your share when we sell the diamonds.'

'I don't care,' said Max, looking more scared than ever and wrenching away from the bigger man. 'You want 'em, you go and get 'em.' He stumbled as he shot off up the beach away from Dave and stood at the bottom of the steps, trembling.

What a cissy, thought George, watching it all from her high window. Fancy being scared of a few waves.

'You wait!' growled Dave as he took off his shoes and socks and waded into the water. He had obviously decided there was nothing for it but to try to get to the steps himself. He climbed up on the first rock as the waves swirled and gurgled around him. The water was waist high and he had a job to keep on his feet as wave after wave broke over the rocks and surged around him.

Suddenly an extra large wave washed over him and he slipped sideways, his arms turning like a windmill as he tried desperately to keep his balance.

Up at the window, George held her breath. She would love to see Dave fall in but if he did and couldn't get to the steps it might mean she would never see Timothy again.

The man recovered his balance and waded slowly the rest of the way to the steps. He climbed up, dripping and shivering with cold.

'All right, kid,' he shouted angrily. 'Throw them down!'

'Not unless you help me climb out first,' called George.

'You'd better!' threatened the burly man. 'Or we'll catch your dog and wring his neck!'

George hesitated, but not for long. She couldn't risk them hurting Timothy. 'Oh, all right, then.' she shouted crossly. 'Here they come!' Reluctantly, she leaned out of the window as far as she could, holding out the package. She dropped it and, to her immense relief, it fell straight into the waiting hands of the robber. He shoved it into his pocket and slowly began to wind his way back across the rocks to safety.

Once on dry land again he took out the package and ripped off the cloth bag. His eyes lit up as he saw the diamonds sparkling in front of him. 'Got 'em, Max,' he called triumphantly.

'Let's have a look,' said Max, running towards him. His eyes lit up too when he saw the jewels.

'Right,' said Dave, pocketing the box and dragging on his socks and shoes. 'Let's get going!'

'Hey, what about me?' yelled George.

But the men didn't seem to hear her. They both ran towards the cliff path as fast as their legs could carry them.

8

Making up stories?

Even though the two robbers were out of sight, George went on hammering on the window and shouting for them to come back. She was furious. How dare they not keep their end of the bargain when she had kept hers!

Suddenly, though, twinkling lights appeared at the top of the cliff, then began to weave down the winding path to the bottom.

George spotted them at once and heaved a huge sigh of relief. Someone was coming. Thank goodness she was going to be rescued at last.

'Help! Help!' she shouted, at the top of her voice.

Two men in coastguard's uniform appeared at the bottom of the path. There was no sign of Dave and Max. They had both completely disappeared. George thought they had probably spotted the coastguards and rushed off across the heather.

'Help,' shouted George from her window. 'I'm trapped up here, please get me out.'

The two coastguards stared up at her in amazement. The last thing they had expected when they saw the light shining out from Rocky Point was a young boy shouting at them from one of the windows.

'What are you doing up there, young lad?' one called. 'This is no place for children to be playing, you know. And how did you manage to light the light?'

'It was easy,' called George anxiously. 'Please help me get out, I've got to find my dog.'

'Dog?' said the other coastguard, looking very puzzled indeed. 'What dog?'

'Timmy,' called George impatiently. 'Did you see him on the way down?'

'No, we didn't see any dog,' said one of the coastguards shaking his head.

'Well, *please* can you help me get out so I can look for him?' shouted George desperately.

By now, the water had calmed down and the coastguards were able to walk across the rocks to the lighthouse steps. Luckily, they were both wearing wellington boots. Once at the steps, the taller man wrenched aside one of the wooden planks nailed across the doorway and produced a huge key from the pocket of his uniform jacket.

'I say, it's mighty stiff,' he said, wincing as he tried to turn the key in the rusty old padlock. 'This place has been shut up for years. I don't know how that boy got in, I'm sure. If it was through the window he must be able to climb like a monkey.'

At last he managed to undo the padlock and, together, the two men heaved open the huge, iron studded door. The rusty old hinges creaked and groaned as it swung back with a clang against the side of the lighthouse. A cool draught of fresh, sea air surged in through the door and up the spiral staircase.

'Oh, thank goodness!' said George, running down to meet them. 'Are you sure you haven't seen my dog?'

'Now, now, young man,' said the taller coastguard taking hold of her arm. 'Never mind about any dog, you've got a lot of explaining to do. How did you get in here, for a start? Don't you know this old lighthouse is dangerous?'

'I didn't get in by myself,' said George indignantly. 'Some robbers *made* me get through the window to look for their diamonds. They said they'd hurt Timothy if I didn't, and now he's disappeared.'

'Now, now, hold your horses,' said the other coastguard looking more puzzled than ever. 'You're not making any sense.'

'Yes, I am!' insisted George indignantly. 'I'll tell you the rest later. I've simply got to find Timmy. He'll be lost and lonely up on the moor and I must go and look for him.' She hurried down the steps and ran across the rocks, not caring if she got her feet wet. Explanations could come later, she *had* to find her beloved puppy.

But the two coastguards hurried after her and caught her arm.

'You'd better tell us where you come from,' said one of them, sounding rather annoyed. 'You'll have some explaining to do to your parents. You're much too young to be out after dark and the police might be interested to hear you've been trespassing in the old lighthouse and messing around with the light. All lighthouses belong to

an organisation called Trinity House, you know, and are private property.'

'Besides,' said the other man. 'It's unsafe and due to be demolished. You've been taking a terrible risk, you know.'

'It wasn't dark when I got here,' said George scowling and not knowing or caring one bit about Trinity House or who lighthouses belonged to or if Rocky Point Lighthouse was going to be knocked down. 'And I come from Kirrin Cottage and I'll go home as soon as I've found my dog.'

'Well, we'll see about that,' said one of the men.

'Yes, we shall,' said George haughtily, feeling more impatient than ever. 'And when I get home I'm going to telephone the police to tell them about the robbers.'

'Stories,' said the tall coastguard shaking his head and taking George's arm. 'Children's stories. Now come on, lad, let's get you home.'

George shook off the man's arm angrily. There was obviously no point in trying to make these men believe her. Grown-ups hardly ever believed what children said. Especially if they were telling them about adventures. They thought only adults had adventures.

With a sigh and a heavy heart, George began to follow the coastguards up the steep path towards the cliff top. It looked as if this was the end of the adventure and it had turned out to be perfectly dreadful. The two robbers must have hidden in the undergrowth then escaped when the coastguards had passed by. Worst of all, darling Timothy had disappeared completely and she might never see him again!

The little girl felt very cold and weary as they reached the top. If Timothy had been hiding in the heather he would have bounded out to meet her by now. What *could* have happened to him?

Then, as she walked, head down, between the two tall men, there unexpectedly came the sound of voices, and more lights appeared coming towards them.

'Hey!' shouted George, running towards the two figures making their way over to them. 'Have you seen my dog?'

As they got closer she saw a pair of burly

policemen leading two dejected-looking figures. They were Dave and Max, caught by the police as they were darting across the moor towards the cliff top road where they had left their van.

'Oh, goody,' said George, when she saw them. 'You've caught them.'

'What do you know about these men, then, young fellow?' asked one of the police officers, looking mighty puzzled.

'Everything,' said George. 'But I'll have to tell you later. I've lost my dog. Have you seen him by any chance? He's small and brown and very shaggy.'

'I haven't seen a dog of any kind,' said the puzzled policeman shaking his head. 'A rabbit or two, but no dogs.'

The coastguards were very surprised indeed to see the police officers. The men stood talking while George hopped from one foot to another impatiently, anxious to be off to search for Timothy.

'We recognised Dave here at once,' the policemen told the coastguards. 'He escaped from prison a few days ago. And the last thing we

expected when someone reported the beam from the old lighthouse was to meet these two villains running off! They insist they didn't light it, so who did?'

'Me,' said George. 'And now you've got the diamonds *and* the thieves perhaps you can help me find my dog, Timothy?'

'Diamonds?' said one of the policeman. 'We haven't found any diamonds. As far as we know the third member of the gang hid them and they've never been found – and he's still in prison.'

'Oh, yes they have been found,' said George, grinning and pointing to an angry-looking Dave. 'He's got them!'

9

Timmy

'Not me,' said the escaped prisoner, as George pointed straight at him, shaking his head firmly. 'I haven't got any diamonds, nor has Max here. This kid doesn't know what he's talking about.'

'Yes I do,' said George angrily, explaining to the policemen and the coastguards what had happened.

'The boy's making up stories,' insisted Max, confirming what his fellow thief had said. 'He didn't find any diamonds and throw them out to us.'

'But it's true,' insisted George angrily. It was only the villains' word against hers. When they saw the policemen coming they must have hidden them somewhere. The trouble was, grown-ups always believed *other* grown-ups and not children, even if the other grown-ups were robbers. 'And what have you done with Timothy,' added the angry and anxious little girl. 'You promised you wouldn't hurt him if I threw you the diamonds, so where *is* he?'

'Haven't seen the wretched mutt,' said Max nastily, shaking his head. 'He ran off.'

'Where?' demanded George.

'Haven't got a clue,' said Max, shrugging again.

'Well, I don't know, I'm sure,' said one of the police officers shaking his head. 'This is all very confusing. But what I do know is that a child your age should be at home with your parents. And *you*,' he added, to the robbers, 'should be locked up. Come on everybody, let's get going.'

'Not until I've found Timothy,' said George stubbornly, staying exactly where she was. 'Timmy! Timmy!' she began calling. 'Where are you?'

'Come on son,' said one of the policeman taking her arm gently. 'We'll escort you home. You can find your dog another time.'

'I'm not going *anywhere* and you can't make me,' said George, rather rudely. 'I *have* to find Timothy.'

But, in spite of her protests, George was led firmly by the arm, along the path across the moor, past Kirrin Farm and the old Mill towards home. The torch beams flashed in front of them, lighting up the path as they went. Once or twice a white bobtail came into view as rabbits scattered in all directions.

George shivered and one of the policemen took off their jacket and put it round her shoulders.

'Thanks,' said George sulkily. She hated leaving without Timothy and imagined him hiding somewhere, cold and scared, wondering what had happened to her. He could even have heard her calling but been too frightened to come in case the horrid men hurt him again.

'We'll take the boy home if you want to get those two back to the police station,' said one of the coastguards as the path forked in two with one way leading to the road, the other taking the direction of Kirrin Cottage.

'Right,' said one policeman. 'We'll call round to Kirrin Cottage later to tell his parents to keep him away from dangerous places.'

But George wasn't listening. She had spied more twinkling lights coming towards them and her sharp ears had caught the sound of a dog barking excitedly. Her heart gave a sudden lurch. She would know that bark anywhere.

All of a sudden, a bundle of brown, shaggy fur hurled itself out of the darkness towards them.

'Timmy!' yelled George, darting forward to meet him. 'Timmy, darling! Thank goodness you're all right!'

'Wuff, wuff!' barked Timothy, his tail wagging so hard it was almost invisible. He flung himself into his small mistress's arms, quivering with joy and licking her face all over.

'Oh, Timmy,' cried George, burying her face in

his soft fur. 'I was so scared I'd never see you again. Where have you been?'

'He's been running home to fetch us,' came a deep voice from the darkness and George's father appeared, flashing his big torch at everyone. 'I say, what on earth's going on? Who are all these people?' he added with a frown. He had been busy in his study working on an important scientific formula when Timothy had arrived home with an old length of rope tied to his collar and barking frantically. He hadn't been at all pleased when George's mother had told him George was missing and that they had to follow Timothy in the hope he would lead them to her. Especially as the dog had come indoors with his paws covered in mud and he had obviously been digging again.

'Oh, George!' cried her mother, hurrying to give her a hug. 'Where *have* you been? We've been so terribly worried about you. And when Timmy turned up on his own we really thought something dreadful had happened to you.'

'It has,' said George, giving her mother a hug in return, more pleased and relieved to see her than she would admit. 'Something dreadfully thrilling.' She began telling them all about the adventure, her words tumbling over one another in her hurry to get them out.

'Oh, for goodness sake, Georgina,' said her father, gazing in bewilderment at the policemen, the coastguards and the villains. 'Stop blabbing and let these grown-ups explain properly.'

'Georgina!' exclaimed one of the coastguards, looking very shocked and surprised indeed. 'We thought she was a young lad!'

'A *girl*!' exclaimed Max. 'Well, I never would have thought it.'

'Oh, that's nothing new. Everyone thinks that,' said George's father, scowling. 'Now perhaps someone will please explain sensibly.'

'We don't know the whole story yet,' said one of the policemen. 'You'd better let your daughter go on.'

It seemed rather strange, standing on top of a windy cliff top with torches flashing all around, recounting a very exciting adventure.

George put Timothy down and he ran off into the heather, snuffling around for interesting things. Rabbits and hedgehogs, hares and toads, they all came out after dark and needed sniffing. He didn't go very far away, though. He had lost his mistress once that day and didn't intend doing so again.

When George paused for breath, her father said. 'Well, you can take my word for it that everything my daughter has told you is true. She might be rather naughty but she never tells lies.'

'Thank you, Father,' said George. 'Wasn't Timmy clever to come and fetch you? Isn't he the cleverest dog in the whole world? How could I ever have thought he was hiding somewhere, too scared to come out!'

'Yes, I suppose he is,' admitted Father. 'He's certainly the noisiest. He barked and barked at us until we followed him up here.'

'And he grabbed your trouser leg and tried to pull you out of the house,' said George's mother with a smile, giving her daughter another big hug for good measure.

'Yes, indeed he did,' said Father, still frowning with his thick, dark eyebrows. 'It's a good thing he didn't tear it, I can tell you!'

'Right,' said the taller of the two policemen, turning to the two villains. 'If, as the professor says, his daughter's story is true . . . *where* are those stolen diamonds?'

'We told you,' insisted Dave in answer to the police officer's query. 'There ain't any diamonds. The kid's lying.'

'I told you, my daughter doesn't tell lies,' said George's father, sticking up for her.

'Anyway, I really don't see how they could have been hidden in the lighthouse,' said one of the coastguards. 'I know Georgina managed to climb inside but the window was far too small for a fully-grown man to get through. This story about the third member of the gang hiding them there seems a bit far-fetched.'

'They said he was very small and could climb like a monkey,' insisted George, scowling fiercely. 'And my name's George.'

'Well, I don't know, I'm sure,' said one of the police officers with a sigh. 'But we can't do anything more now,' he added, giving the two thieves a push. 'Come on you two, down to the Station. I'll collect my jacket tomorrow,' he said to George as she still had it round her shoulders. 'Now you get on home and have a good night's sleep.'

'Thank you for rescuing my daughter,' said Father to the coastguards as they said goodbye. 'I'll make sure she doesn't get into any more scrapes.' He shook his head in bewilderment. 'Climbing into the lighthouse and setting the light, I don't know I'm sure.'

Secretly, the professor was rather proud of his daughter being clever enough to think of doing such a thing, but he would never admit that to her.

'It wasn't a scrape, Father,' insisted George indignantly as they set off for home. 'It was an adventure.'

'Hmph,' snorted her father. 'Well, will you please not let your adventures interfere with my work in future, young lady.'

George scowled again. She hated being called a young lady almost as much as she hated being called Georgina!

'Come along, then, dear,' said her mother, taking hold of her hand. 'Let's get home. You must be very hungry. Joanna has left some lovely homemade vegetable soup for you.'

'Mmm, goody,' said George, suddenly realising she was starving. It was hours and *hours* since she had had anything to eat. Timothy must be hungry too, running to and fro across the moor. His stomach must be rumbling like thunder.

'Timmy! Come along, we're going now,' called George, as Timothy came bounding from the undergrowth.

'Just look at him!' said Father, shining his torch

at the puppy. 'I do believe he's been digging again!'

'Oh, Timmy,' said George, laughing and giving the shaggy little dog a hug. 'You just can't resist it, can you?'

'Wuff,' said Timothy happily. 'Wuff, wuff!'

10

A puzzle

They were all soon back at Kirrin Cottage. Timothy wolfed down his dinner and George sat at the kitchen table swallowing spoonfuls of Joanna's delicious homemade soup with chunks of crusty bread dripping with butter.

Father had gone to get on with some important work in his study and George's mother was brushing the floor where Timothy had walked mud all over the mat.

'That was lovely,' said George, sitting back when she had finished her supper and giving a huge yawn. 'I say, I'm jolly tired.'

'I'm not surprised, after such an exciting day,' said her mother. 'I think it's time you went to bed, don't you?'

'I suppose so,' said George, getting down from the table and washing up her bowl and spoon. 'Look, Timmy's sleepy too,' she added with a smile as Timothy gave a yawn and showed his rows of sharp little teeth. 'Adventures always make him tired.'

George fluffed up the blanket in the dog basket by the stove and Timothy climbed in. He turned round and round three or four times, then lay down with a sigh, gazing up at George from under his shaggy eyebrows.

'I'll be down for you later as usual,' whispered George in the puppy's ear as she gave him a hug and a kiss goodnight. Timothy was not really allowed upstairs on her bed but every night when her parents had gone to sleep she crept down and

took him up to her room. She couldn't bear to think of him all alone in the big kitchen. Luckily, no-one ever suspected as she brought Timothy back downstairs before anyone else woke up in the morning.

'Wurf,' said Timothy sleepily, his eyes opening and closing. He really was a very tired puppy. He had had a most exciting day. The most exciting he could remember for a long time.

George went upstairs to get undressed. She

climbed on to her bed and looked out of the window. The light from Rocky Point Lighthouse was still shining out through the darkness.

'I wonder how long it will stay lit,' she said to herself, giving a chuckle when she thought how surprised everyone must have been to see the old lighthouse shining its light out across the sea after all those years. Her plan had worked brilliantly. Better than she could ever have hoped.

Even though she was very tired indeed, George tossed and turned in her bed, her mind going over the exciting events of the day. Outside, she could hear the swishing of the waves as they broke on the sand and the hoot of an owl in the orchard. There was something still mystifying her very much indeed. Something she had been puzzling over ever since the police officers turned up at Rocky Point with the two thieves held firmly by the arms.

Where *were* those diamonds?

'I saw that horrid Dave catch them,' she whispered to herself. 'So I know they had them with them when they ran off. I threw them from the lighthouse window straight into his hands.'

But when the policemen bumped into the villains hurrying away over the cliff top as fast as they could, there had been no sign of the box wrapped in a brown bag.

'It's a real mystery,' said George, frowning into the darkness. 'What on earth did they do with them?'

The little girl lay listening for her parents' footsteps on the stairs. When she heard them go to their room she waited a while, then slipped down to get Timothy.

'I just can't think what they could have done with the diamonds, Timmy,' she said as they tip-toed back up the stairs. 'Can you?'

'Wurf,' said Timothy, jumping on to her bed and snuggling down in his usual place. At that particular moment he didn't really care about the diamonds. All he cared about was being home safe and sound with George.

'Surely they wouldn't have thrown them away?' said George in a puzzled whisper. 'Not after all the trouble they went to get them.'

'Wuff,' said Timothy, closing his eyes sleepily. Then he opened them again as George went on.

'Perhaps they threw the box into the heather and intend coming back for it?' she suggested.

'Wuff,' said Timothy, giving another yawn.

'Although I'm sure they'll both go to prison, so it's going to be a long time before they can come back to look for them,' said George, tossing and turning, trying to get comfortable.

'Wuff,' said Timothy, very sleepily indeed. He really did want to get some rest and quite wished George would stop talking to him.

'That horrid Dave will definitely be locked up,' continued George. 'Because he was in prison in the first place. But I'm not sure the policemen will be able to prove the other man is a robber if they don't have the stolen diamonds as evidence.' She sat up suddenly, almost tipping Timothy off the end of the bed. 'Oh, Timmy, darling! Do you realise we've simply got to find them otherwise they might let that horrible Max go and he'll come back to get us!' 'Wuff,' said Timothy, deciding that if he kept on agreeing with his mistress she might eventually decide to settle down and go to sleep.

After all, he really didn't know *what* she was worrying about!

George managed to get to sleep at last, in spite of the puzzle spinning round in her head.

'We'll get up first thing, Timmy,' she murmured sleepily as her eyes closed and she dozed off. 'Don't forget now . . . first thing!'

But Timothy didn't answer this time. He was fast asleep, his nose and ears twitching as he chased rabbits in his sleep.

11

Timothy digs again

When George woke up, the sun was streaming through her window. The sky was a brilliant blue, with one or two cotton-wool clouds drifting along the horizon. The sea was as calm as a mirror.

She jumped out of bed and hurried down the stairs with Timothy before anyone else was awake.

She opened the back door and let him out for a run in the garden. Joanna was just coming along the garden path.

'Oh, I *am* pleased to see you, George!' exclaimed the kindly woman when she saw George standing there in her pyjamas. 'We did wonder where you'd got to yesterday. Your poor mother was worried sick!'

'We had an adventure,' said George, calling Timothy and going back indoors. 'I was trapped in a lighthouse and Timothy was kidnapped by robbers.'

'Well, what an imagination you've got,' laughed Joanna. 'But you should always be home before dark, you know, whatever game you're playing.'

'It wasn't my imagination,' said George, with a scowl. 'And you can't come home if you're stuck in a lighthouse, can you?'

'No, dear,' said Joanna, still smiling. 'Now run along and get dressed while I cook you a nice breakfast.'

George was quite used to grown-ups not believing her when she told them about her adventures so she ran quickly upstairs and pulled on her shorts and shirt. She hadn't forgotten her pledge to go back to Rocky Point to search for the diamonds.

'Mmm, lovely, I'm starving. Thank you, Joanna,' she said, a little while later, as the housekeeper put a huge plate of bacon, eggs, sausage and fried bread in front of her. 'We're off to find the jewels this morning, aren't we, Timmy?'

'Wurf,' agreed Timothy from under the table where he was chewing his beefy breakfast biscuits.

'Well, well,' said Joanna, grinning. 'More adventures, then?'

'That's right,' said George, her mouth full of delicious crunchy fried bread.

'Would you like to take a picnic?' asked Joanna. 'Searching for jewels can make you very hungry.'

'Oh, yes, please,' said George, swallowing the last of her breakfast and finishing the glass of creamy milk that Joanna had placed beside her plate.

'Now you be back before dark this time,' said Joanna with a smile as she packed a delicious picnic of cheese sandwiches, rosy tomatoes, a slice of homemade chocolate cake and a bottle of ginger pop into George's rucksack. 'Your poor mother will worry herself to death if you're late home again.'

'We promise,' said George, shrugging on her rucksack and calling to Timothy. 'See you later,' she added with a wave of her hand as she hurried out of the back door and down the garden path. Her heart thumped excitedly. It was wonderful to be off on another adventure on such a grand morning.

Although it was very early, it was already warm. George could feel the sun shining on her skin and smell the salty tang of the sea air.

'Come on, Timmy,' she called as he sniffed around the flower beds. 'There's no time to go digging again.'

'Wuff,' said Timothy, scampering after her. Hurrah, they were going on another adventure! 'Wuff, wuff!'

Up the path the two went, and along the cliff top, following the way they had come the evening before. Timothy scampered on ahead, sniffing and snuffling in the heather for exciting smells. His tail waved in the air like a shaggy banner. He remembered sniffing and snuffling up here not all that long ago when it was quite dark. Sniffing and snuffling and digging.

'This way, Timmy,' called George as Timothy disappeared into the heather. All she could see was his tail sticking up. 'Don't get lost now, we've got to look for those diamonds!'

They soon passed Kirrin Farm and the old Mill and began to descend the steep path towards Rocky Point Lighthouse. Timothy ran on ahead, then dived into the undergrowth. George soon realised he had disappeared completely.

'Timmy,' she called. 'I'm going down to search among the rocks!'

Down the stony track she scrambled until she came to the small beach. The tide was low and it was easy to step across to the lighthouse.

'The oil must be all burned up,' she said, gazing upwards and noticing that the light had gone out. 'I suppose the lighthouse will be knocked down very soon and it will never shine again. It's very sad, isn't it, Timmy, old boy?'

When there was no answering woof from him she looked round with a frown on her face. Where had that naughty puppy got to? He was supposed to be helping her look for the package of precious diamonds.

She clambered on to the rocks and peered into all the nooks and crannies. She peered into rock pools where tiny shrimps swam and scarlet sea anemones waved their fingers at her as the breeze rippled the water. She scrambled round the ledge on the side of the lighthouse but there was no sign of anything.

'I don't really suppose they were silly enough to hide the box here, anyway,' she muttered impatiently to herself. 'It would have been washed away by the tide.' She stepped back on to the beach and stood with her hands on her hips and a frown on her face. *Where* in the world could the box be? It simply must be around here somewhere!

At last she decided to look further up the path. After all, the villains had been some way up before the policemen had collared them.

'Yes!' she said, with a sudden surge of excitement. 'That's it! They hid it somewhere along the path.'

But where? The track wound up the side of the cliff and it would have been too dangerous to step off it in the dark to hide something amongst the boulders. And at the top were acres of heather and bracken that stretched as far as the eye could see.

George gave a sigh. It would be like looking for a needle in a haystack.

On she went, though, determined not to give up. Once George set her mind to something, she *never* gave up. She scrambled up the path, head down, looking for a likely hiding place, when she suddenly realised she hadn't seen Timothy for ages.

'Timmy!' she called in a very loud voice. 'I'm going back up. Where are you?'

She looked up and saw the little dog sitting on the path a little way ahead, his pink tongue hanging out and his tail wagging nineteen to the dozen. For some strange reason, he was looking very pleased with himself.

'There you are,' panted George as she got closer. 'What *have* you been doing. Not chasing rabbits, I hope!'

Then George saw exactly what Timothy had been doing. He had been digging again. His paws were black from the peaty soil and his nose was covered in mud. But, in spite of all that, he looked happy and proud and very excited about something. So excited he was quivering all over.

'Wuff,' he barked. 'Wuff, wuff!'

As George reached Timothy she saw why he was looking so pleased with himself. At his feet lay a small brown bag with something inside. A box. A box containing a priceless diamond necklace!

12

The end of the adventure

George dropped to her knees and picked up the box. 'Timmy, you clever, darling dog! Where on earth did you find it?' she gasped.

'Wuff,' barked Timothy, running back into the heather. 'Wuff, wuff!' he barked over his shoulder. *Follow me and I'll show you*.

George picked up the box and waded after him.

The heather was rough and scratchy and tore at her knees but she didn't care one bit. She had to see where Timothy had found the jewels.

The little dog had stopped at a place where there was a clearing in the heather. There were a few little grassy mounds in the damp earth covered with a carpet of wild flowers. Cowslips and dainty blue harebells nodded their pretty heads in the breeze. Beside the grassy mounds there was a deep hole. A hole Timothy had dug the night before to bury the box of jewels!

'Oh, Timmy!' cried George in awe and wonderment when she saw it. She crouched down and hugged Timothy so tightly she almost strangled him. 'Dave must have chucked the box into the heather and you found it and buried it. You clever, clever, thing. No wonder you arrived home covered in dirt. You stopped to bury it before you ran to get Mummy and Father. You clever, darling dog!' She hugged him again and gave him a resounding kiss on the top of his shaggy head.

'Wuff, wuff,' said Timothy, in rather a strangled voice. His tail wagged furiously. Pleasing his dear mistress was the nicest thing in the whole wide world, even if she *did* almost choke him afterwards!

'Come on!' cried George, when she had finished hugging and kissing him. 'Let's get back and tell Mummy and she can ring the police station. I wouldn't be surprised if you get a medal for this, Timmy. You're the cleverest dog in the world!'

The excited little girl and her dog were soon hurrying back to Kirrin Cottage as fast as they possibly could.

'My, my,' cried Joanna in surprise as the two hurtled through the back door. 'You weren't gone very long. Surely you haven't eaten all that food already? Oh, and by the way, did you find the diamonds?' she added with a chuckle.

'Yes, we jolly well did,' exclaimed George, yanking the box out of her rucksack. 'What do you think of these, then?'

Joanna's mouth fell open in surprise as George unwrapped the box and carefully opened it up. The woman gasped when she saw the two rows

of sparkling diamonds in front of her. 'Well, I never,' she said, sitting down very suddenly. 'Well, I never did!'

Soon George's parents were staring at the diamonds too. Her mother came in just as George was showing Joanna and was so thrilled that she called Father from his study immediately.

'My word,' said Father, when he heard how Timothy had buried them when the robbers had thrown them into the heather so the police wouldn't discover them. 'I never thought that dog's dreadful habit of digging would come in useful.'

'Wurf,' said Timothy as if to say that digging was *always* useful.

'You'd better telephone the police station, Quentin,' said George's mother. 'They'll be very pleased indeed to hear we've found the jewels.'

'You mean, *Timmy's* found them, Mummy!' said George indignantly, giving her puppy another big hug.

'All right,' laughed her mother. '*Timmy's* found them.'

'Do you think he'll get a medal?' asked George, as they waited for her father to return from using the telephone.

'Well, he certainly deserves one,' said Joanna, laughing.

'PC Moon is coming for the diamonds right away,' said Father returning to the kitchen. 'He's very pleased, as you can imagine.'

'I hope you're pleased too, Father,' said George gazing up at the stern man.

'Of course I am,' said her father. 'But I would still rather you didn't get into these scrapes,

George. And just because Timothy went digging on the moor it does *not* mean he can dig up your mother's garden, you know.'

'Wuff,' said Timothy, sitting meekly at George's feet. He simply couldn't understand why humans didn't realise dogs just had to dig sometimes.

'He won't honestly,' said George gazing down at her puppy. 'Look, he's as good as gold.'

'And he'd better stay that way,' said her father, trying to frown but only managing a smile instead.

'He can stay here, then?' said George, her vivid eyes twinkling. 'And you won't ask PC Moon to find him another home?'

'Well . . .' said her father.

'Oh, Father, you couldn't possibly send him away when he's such a hero,' insisted George.

'I suppose not,' said her father reluctantly, as they heard PC Moon's car draw up outside the front door. 'But woe betide him if he gets into mischief again.' He waggled his finger at Timothy. 'Do you hear that, dog?'

'Wuff,' said Timothy, ignoring him and running to the front door when he heard PC Moon's

knock. 'Wuff, wuff, wuff!' He knew dogs were supposed to bark when someone knocked at the door. Now he was in Father's good books, he had better make sure he stayed that way!

The little dog felt very happy and satisfied as he waited for Father to open the front door and let the police officer in to collect the diamonds. What an exciting adventure this had been and what a lucky fellow Timothy was to live at Kirrin Cottage by the lovely sea with a little girl like George!

What other dog in the whole wide world had a mistress who had as many thrilling adventures as she did?